NATASHA WING'S The Night
the New Pet

Grosset & Dunlap
An Imprint of Penguin Random House

To All Aboard Animal Rescue and Shelter, and animal
foster care people, like Kristi Ross, who have big hearts and
help save and find homes for animals. Thank you!—NW

For Loki, the newest four-legged member of the family—AW

GROSSET & DUNLAP
Penguin Young Readers Group
An Imprint of Penguin Random House LLC

Text copyright © 2016 by Natasha Wing. Illustrations copyright © 2016 by Penguin Random House LLC. All rights reserved.
Published by Grosset & Dunlap, an imprint of Penguin Random House LLC, 345 Hudson Street, New York, New York 10014.
GROSSET & DUNLAP is a trademark of Penguin Random House LLC. Manufactured in China.

Library of Congress Cataloging-in-Publication Data is available.

ISBN 978-0-448-48903-2   10 9 8 7 6 5 4 3 2 1

NATASHA WING'S The Night Before
the New Pet

By Natasha Wing

Illustrated by Amy Wummer

Grosset & Dunlap
An Imprint of Penguin Random House

'Twas the night before we got a pet,
and all through the house,
all the chew toys were scattered.
Squeak! went a rubber mouse.

The fleece bed was set
in my bedroom with care.

Soon a sweet little puppy
will be sleeping right there.

We went to the pet store
to buy a collar and a leash.

"Need a few treats?" asked the clerk.
Mom said, "We'll take some of each."

My sister wants a pony,
but we're getting a pup.

"Let's get two pets!" she begged.
She just wouldn't give up.

How about a gray bunny?

Or a snow-white chinchilla?

"Pleeeease!" said my sister.
"We could name it Vanilla!"

"It's settled," said Dad.
"One pet is enough."

"Then I get to name it.
I'll call it Snugglefluff."

That night we nestled all snug in our beds,

while visions of wagging tails danced in our heads.

Early the next morning,
Dad set up the crate.
I put in a blanket and cried,
"Oh, I can't wait!"

We drove to the shelter.
There were animals galore!
Gerbils and pygmy goats . . .

Oops! One piddled on the floor.

There were all kinds of dogs,
from big ones to small.
Of course my sister insisted
she wanted them all!

Then what to our wondering eyes should appear
but a frisky little pooch with one floppy ear.

His fur was so soft.
His nose—cold and wet.
He was the cutest pup ever . . .

the perfect new pet!

"He's a great dog," said the lady.
"And he's part Yorkshire terrier."
"Let's take him home," I said.
Dad put him in the carrier.

We were about to leave
when we heard a *me-ew*.
"Oh, please! She's so cute.
Can't we bring her home, too?"

Dad picked up the kitten.
She started to purr.

"Hello, precious," he cooed
to the tiny ball of fur.

What a total surprise
to see Dad so smitten.

Guess what happened next . . .

We brought home a dog and a kitten!